Goose Girl

Written by Joe McLellan and Matrine McLellan

Illustrated by Rhian Brynjolson

PEMMICAN
PUBLICATIONS
INC.

Pemmican Publications gratefully acknowledges the assistance accorded to its publishing program by the Manitoba Arts Council, the Province of Manitoba – Department of Culture, Heritage and Tourism, Canada Council for the Arts and Canadian Heritage – Book Publishing Industry Development Program.

Printed and Bound in Canada.
First Printing: 2007   Second Printing: 2008   Third Printing: 2009   Fourth Printing: 2012   Fifth Printing: 2015

Library and Archives Canada Cataloguing in Publication

McLellan, Joseph
    Goose girl/written by Joe McLellan and Matrine
McLellan illustrated by Rhian Brynjolson

ISBN: 978-1-894717-44-1

    1. Geese–Juvenile fiction. 2. Cree Indians—Juvenile fiction.
    3. Canada, Northern—Juvenile fiction. I. Brynjolson, Rhian
    II. McLellan, Matrine, 1946- III. Title

PS8575.L454G66 2007   jC813'.6   C2007-904571-5

PEMMICAN PUBLICATIONS INC.
Committed to the promotion of Metis culture and heritage

150 Henry Avenue, Winnipeg, Manitoba   R3B 0J7, Canada

www.pemmicanpublications.ca

Dedicated to Sierra – from Joe

With thanks to Jocelyn Bruyere for lending her
expertise in the Cree language, and to
Randal McIlroy for his careful editorial shepherding.

To my Dianna – from Matrine

For my family, and for my students and
colleagues at Wellington School
– from Rhian

Many years ago, by a lake in Northern Canada, there lived a girl named Marie. She spoke French and she spoke Cree.

Every evening in the fall, Marie walked to the lake to watch the geese land.

Marie loved the geese.

She loved them with her whole heart.

Marie thought that geese were the most beautiful creatures in the whole world. They were her family. They were her friends.

They were her babies.

There were hunters at the lake too. Every time that Marie heard their guns roar, and saw a beautiful goose fall dead from the sky, her whole body would shudder and she would cry.

Marie didn't hate the hunters. Her father and brothers were hunters. Marie knew that they had to hunt geese for their family to survive. On evenings when they had goose for supper, Marie would sit in another part of the house and her mother would bring her something else to eat. Her mother understood.

Marie loved the fall.

The way that night came so quickly, bringing with it a chill that turned her breath into a cold mist that would rise to the moon. She loved the rustle that her feet made as she walked through the fallen leaves on her way to the lake.

When she looked up into the sky she would see a small black dot that would move closer until it exploded into an uneven vee of flying singing geese, who would circle down and land on her lake for the night.

Marie could only count to 100, but she was sure that thousands of geese landed on her lake every night.

One evening, while she was watching her geese, Marie felt her mother walk up behind her. They stood silently and watched the geese until her mother softly rested her hand on Marie's shoulder and whispered into her ear.

"Ni danis, my daughter, when we die the geese take our spirits south into the sky to our promised land."

"That's what I was thinking, ma mere, my mother," said Marie as she reached up to take her mother's hand.

They walked home silently in the moonlight listening to the geese singing on the lake.

One night right after her 10th birthday, Marie heard a noise behind her as she walked home from the lake. When she got to her house she turned and saw that a particular goose had followed her home.

They looked into each other's eyes for the longest time until Marie turned and entered her house and the goose flew back to the lake. After that, the same goose followed her home every night, and every night they stood and looked into each other's eyes.

Her dad and her brothers loved to tease Marie,
but even they knew not to tease her about the
goose that followed her home.

After Marie had said her prayers and gone to bed one night, her mother came and sat on the edge of her bed. She brushed the hair back from Marie's eyes, the way mothers always do, and said:

"Mishoom, Grandfather, has told us to call you Niskaw now. If you like that name we will have a feast for it and it will be yours forever."

Marie lay silently for minutes, then sat up and hugged her mother tightly.

"I love it, ma mere, my mother, I just love it."

Over and over, as she fell to sleep that night Marie whispered:

"Niskaw, Niskaw, Niskaw, Niskaw," the Cree word for goose.

Two weeks later, everyone went to Mishoom's house after Mass. Mishoom had set out a feast on a blanket in the yard. They had buffalo, venison, moose, whitefish, pickerel, onions, potatoes, carrots, bannock, berries, pies and tea. Before they could eat, one of Marie's brothers took a little of each food and placed it on a small plate. He placed a small offering of tobacco on the plate too and asked Mishoom to pray over it and bless the food.

When they had finished eating Mishoom called Marie to him.

"Astum, Marie, astum, come, Marie come."

He took her hands in his, the way grandfathers often do, and looked deeply into her eyes.

"From now on," he said to her, "we will call you Niskaw. The goose that follows you home has shown us this name. It is your spirit name that your family will know and you will tell to those that you love.

"You will still be Marie, but Niskaw makes you more than Marie. It makes you able to bring the teachings and the healings of the geese to our people.

"Come with me, granddaughter."

23

They took the plate with the blessed food and walked to the cemetery.

"Sit here, Niskaw, this is my father's grave."

Mishoom fed Niskaw from the plate that they had brought.

"Eat this," Mishoom said, "for your ancestors. The geese have taken their spirits to the promised land. You will do their work now and the work of the geese. This is how you will help our people."

Mishoom took the tobacco from the plate and put Niskaw's hand on his. Together they placed the tobacco on the grave as an offering to their ancestors.

It was still dark the next morning when she heard Mishoom calling her. "Hurry, Niskaw, before the light, let's go. We must get to the lake before daybreak."

Niskaw threw on her dress over her nightclothes and ran outside. She took Mishoom's hand and they hurried to the lake as fast as an old man and a young girl can go. When they reached the shore, Mishoom took a handful of tobacco from his pouch and gave it to her.

"Put this on the water, Niskaw, as an offering to your brothers and sisters, the geese."

She did this carefully. Immediately, the geese began to fly off toward the south. She watched them go one at a time for over an hour.

Finally one last goose, her goose, swam directly in front of Niskaw. She and the goose looked into each other's eyes for a long, long time until the goose turned and flew off to join the others.

Niskaw turned and saw all of her relatives standing on the shore next to her Mishoom. Each one of them came to her in turn, shook her hand, hugged her, kissed her on her cheek and whispered, "Niskaw," her new name, into her ear. Even her brothers did so.

From that day on, Niskaw dreamed of geese every night.

In the morning, after breakfast, she would sit at the table with her mother and her kokoom, her grandmother who lived with them. They would talk about her dreams.

One August day, Niskaw's mother said:

"Come, ni danis, we must visit Mishoom."

When they got to Mishoom's house, they found him in bed. Niskaw took her Mishoom's hand.

"I'm dying, my Niskaw, I'm dying," he told her.

Niskaw pulled a chair next to his bed and sat holding his hand. She wiped his forehead when he perspired, and when he cried out in pain, she kissed his cheek and whispered:

"Fais-do-do, ni mishoom, fais-do-do, go to sleep, my grandfather, go to sleep," just like you would say to a little baby.

Niskaw stayed for days and days holding Mishoom's hand and comforting him.

One morning the room became very bright. Mishoom opened his eyes and looked into hers for a long, long time.

"Kinanaskomitin, ni Niskaw, kinanaskomitin, thank you, my Niskaw, thank you," he whispered, as his hand tumbled from hers.

Niskaw hurried to the table and took some tobacco from Mishoom's pouch. She ran to the lake and spread the tobacco on the water. All of the geese on the lake turned toward her. Her goose came away from the flock. It swam right up to her and looked into her eyes. She held its gaze for the longest time then said:

"Take Mishoom's spirit to our ancestors, south to the promised land."

The geese all rose and flew off to the south. Niskaw began to slowly walk back to her house, as her goose turned in the air, landed on the shore and followed her home. When she reached home, Niskaw sat down on the ground and hung her head. Her goose hopped into her lap and nestled into her chest. Niskaw wrapped her arms around her goose and buried her face into its soft feathery back and cried harder than she had ever cried in her whole life. When she stopped, her goose hopped down and flew back to the lake. The door opened behind her and she heard her mother say:

"Pepihtikwe, iskwesis, pepihtikwe, come in, my girl, come in."

Niskaw grew to be an old woman. Every day for the rest of her life she visited the sick, comforted the dying and called the geese to take their spirits home.

On her last day on earth, when she was a very old woman, she walked out into the blazing sun with her cane to the lake, sat on the sand on her shore and called once to the geese. Her goose swam away from the flock and came right up to where the water meets the sand. It looked up and they gazed lovingly into each other's eyes for the longest, longest time. Until, old Niskaw, she lay her cane down on the sand, and she and her goose flew away together, forever.